You're Snug With Me

Chitra Soundar & Poonam Mistry

LANTANA PUBLISHING

When the willows turned
crimson, Mama Bear dug
into the snow drifts not
far from the sea.

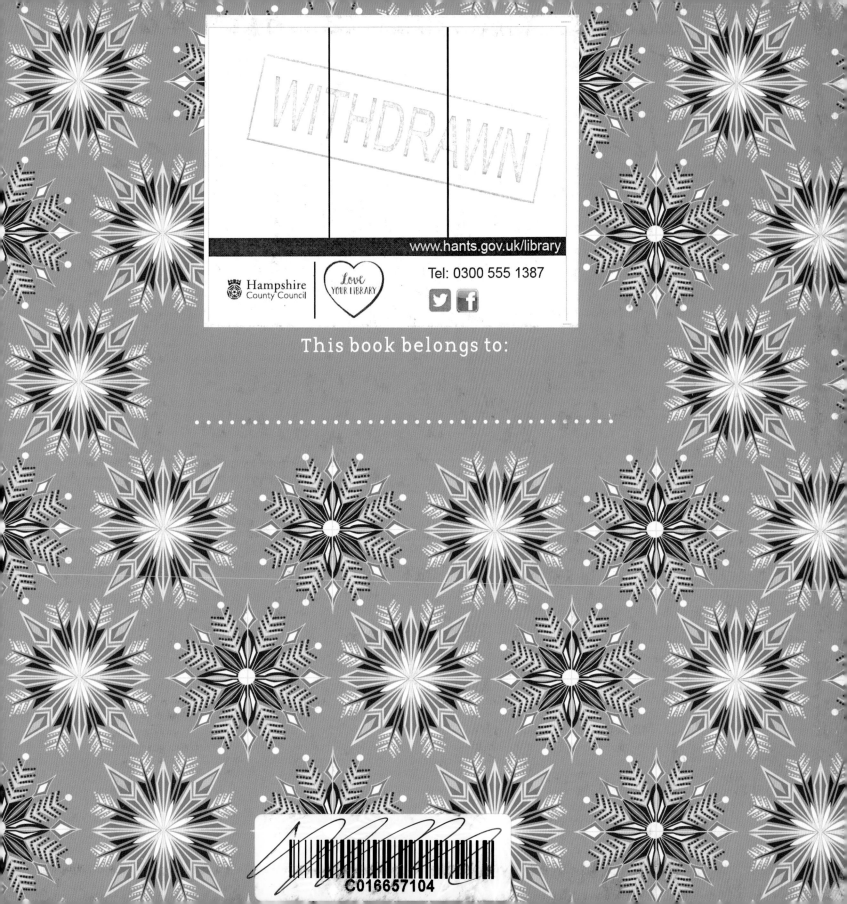

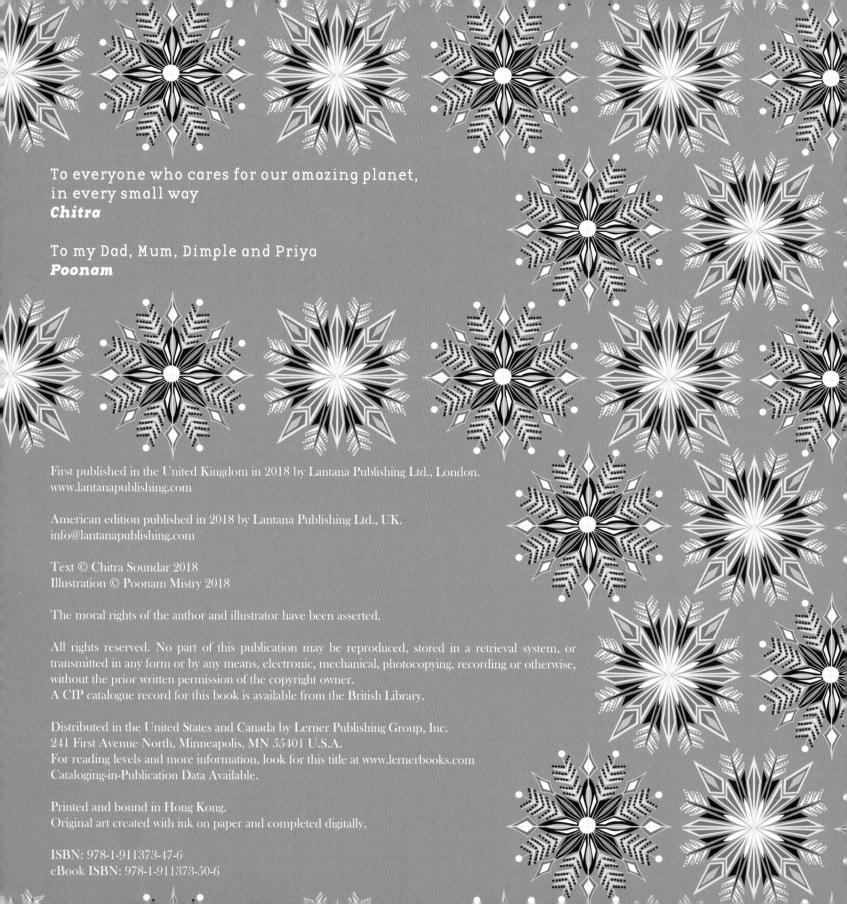

To everyone who cares for our amazing planet,
in every small way
Chitra

To my Dad, Mum, Dimple and Priya
Poonam

First published in the United Kingdom in 2018 by Lantana Publishing Ltd., London.
www.lantanapublishing.com

American edition published in 2018 by Lantana Publishing Ltd., UK.
info@lantanapublishing.com

Text © Chitra Soundar 2018
Illustration © Poonam Mistry 2018

Distributed in the United States and Canada by Lerner Publishing Group, Inc.
241 First Avenue North, Minneapolis, MN 55401 U.S.A.
For reading levels and more information, look for this title at www.lernerbooks.com
Cataloging-in-Publication Data Available.

Printed and bound in Hong Kong.
Original art created with ink on paper and completed digitally.

ISBN: 978-1-911373-47-6
eBook ISBN: 978-1-911373-50-6

She made a den just big
enough for her to turn over,
and waited for the falling
snow to seal it shut.

As the cold set in, she gave birth to two bear cubs. They couldn't see or hear anything yet, but soon they grew.

"Hush!" whispered Mama Bear.
"You're snug with me."

As winter turned colder, the cubs
explored their frozen den. "Mama,
what lies beyond here?" they asked.

"Above us is a land of ice and
snow," said Mama Bear.

The cubs shivered.

"Don't be afraid," said Mama Bear.
"The drifts bring us hard snow,
so we can safely walk this land."

"Can we wander where we please?" asked the cubs.

"Only where the land will let us walk," Mama Bear replied.

"But hush now, you're snug with me."

As the nights grew longer,
the cubs turned restless.
"What lies beyond the ice and
snow?" they asked.

"Beyond the snow is the
ocean," said Mama Bear. "It is
full of ice from long ago."

The cubs shuddered.

"Don't be afraid," said Mama
Bear. "As long as the ice stays
frozen, we will never go
hungry."

"Will the ice melt?" asked the cubs.

"Only if we don't take care of it,"
Mama Bear replied.

"But hush now, you're snug with me."

As the snow fell harder, the cubs grew curious. "Will it always be dark?" they asked.

"It is dark because we are far from the sun during the winter months."

The cubs trembled.

"Don't be afraid," said Mama Bear. "The Earth dances on her toes and when she tilts, our nights will get shorter and spring will return."

"What if the Earth falls down?" asked the cubs.

"She has never faltered in her steps before," Mama Bear replied.

"But hush now, you're snug with me."

As lights dazzled in the polar sky, the cubs wondered about the world outside. "Will we be alone on the snow?" they asked.

"We're never alone in this world," said Mama Bear. "We share the land with foxes and snowshoe hares. Whales, seals and walruses swim in our seas. Terns and geese fly through the skies."

The cubs gasped.

"Don't be afraid," said Mama Bear. "We are the biggest and bravest of all the creatures on the ice."

"Is everything ours then?" asked the cubs.

"We should only ever take what we need," replied Mama Bear.

"But hush now, you're snug with me."

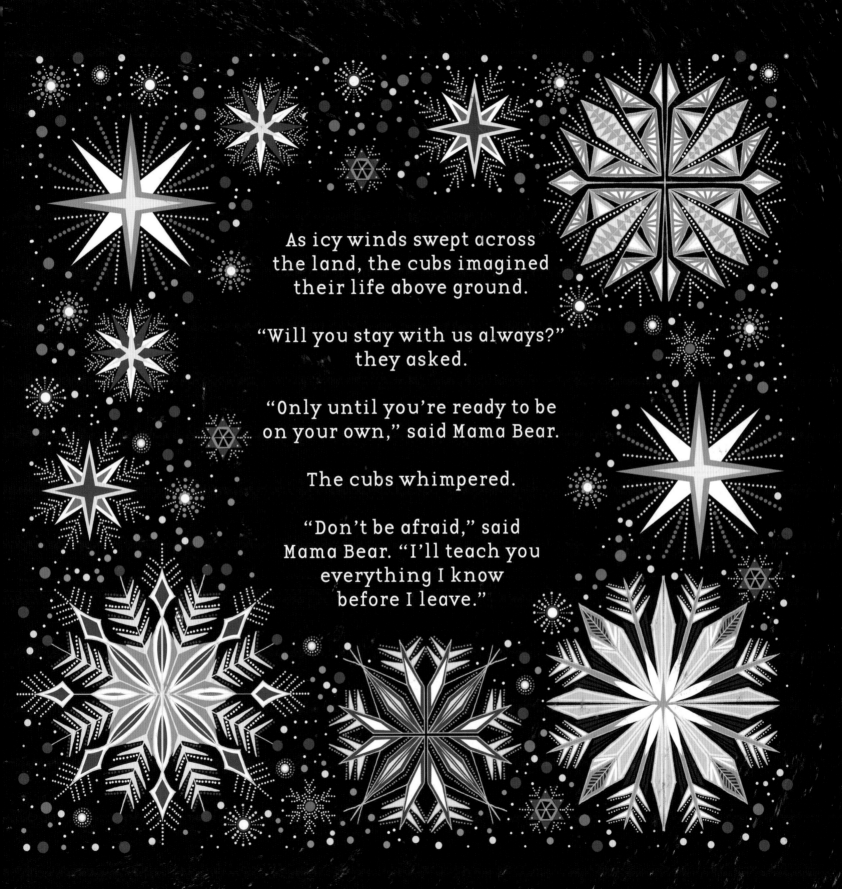

As icy winds swept across
the land, the cubs imagined
their life above ground.

"Will you stay with us always?"
they asked.

"Only until you're ready to be
on your own," said Mama Bear.

The cubs whimpered.

"Don't be afraid," said
Mama Bear. "I'll teach you
everything I know
before I leave."

"What if we don't want to be on our own?" the cubs asked.

"You'll find a friend when you need one,"
Mama Bear replied.

"But hush now, you're
snug with me."

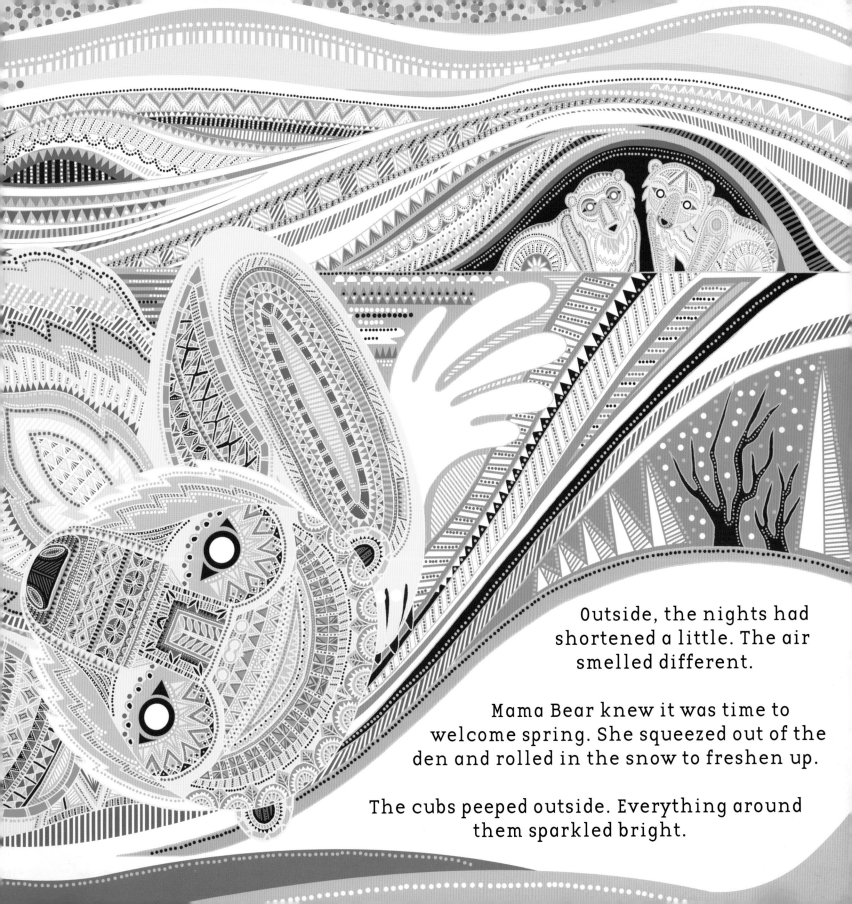

Outside, the nights had shortened a little. The air smelled different.

Mama Bear knew it was time to welcome spring. She squeezed out of the den and rolled in the snow to freshen up.

The cubs peeped outside. Everything around them sparkled bright.

"Don't be afraid,"
called Mama Bear.

They clambered up, slipping and stumbling
on the snow to reach her.

Mama Bear watched her cubs take their first steps on the snow and whispered,

"You're snug with me."

Dear reader,

I wrote this book to show the wonders of our polar lands. This is where we find the pristine white of snow, the trembling blue of sea and the shimmering green and pink of the Northern Lights.

This is where we find the majestic polar bears, the largest land carnivores. Did you know that polar bear cubs are no bigger than guinea pigs when they are born? Although the Arctic is very cold, a layer of fat under the polar bears' skin – called blubber – keeps them warm. Polar bears have black skin to soak up heat from the sun, and their hollow fur only appears white because it reflects light from the snow. In fact, if polar bears were made to live in hot climates, their fur would grow algae and turn green!

This book is more than a story about Mama Bear and her two curious cubs. Like the young cubs, I hope that you and other children who read it will understand that this natural world is our only home. Even if we are the mightiest predator on this planet, we don't live alone and should only ever take what we need.

I hope this story inspires you to be curious about where you live and with whom you share these lands, skies and oceans. And above all, I hope we can all work together to care for this awe-inspiring planet that is our home.

Chitra